Published by Oren Village, LLC, Battle Creek, Michigan. For information or permission to reproduce, please contact author@alanstjean.com or write to Alan St. Jean, PO Box 1, Battle Creek, Michigan 49016. Text set in Baskerville. Cover design by Libby Carruth Krock. Illustrations were rendered in watercolor and pencil.

PUBLISHER'S CATLOGING-IN-PUBLICATION DATA

St. Jean, Alan.

Big fella / written by Alan St. Jean ; illustrated by Libby Carruth Krock. -- 1st ed. -- Battle Creek, Mich. : Oren Village, c2008.

p. ; cm.

(The daydreams collection ; v. 1)

ISBN: 978-0-9777272-2-3
Audience: grades K-5.
Summary: Ralphie learns valuable lessons about cooperation as he wanders through the jungle of his imagination in pursuit of a great big lion.

.

1. Cooperation--Juvenile fiction. 2. Interpersonal relations--Juvenile fiction. 3. Imagination--Juvenile fiction.
4. [Cooperativeness--Fiction. 5. Fantasy.] 6. Fantasy fiction.
I. Krock, Libby Carruth. II. Title. III. Series.

PZ7.S14245 B54 2008
[Fic]--dc22   0810

Oren Village

For Brooks.
What great imagination adventures we had together.
May they never end...

-Alan St. Jean

*

For my dad, George.
Thank you for inspiring me to be a dreamer.

-Libby Carruth Krock

BIG FELLA

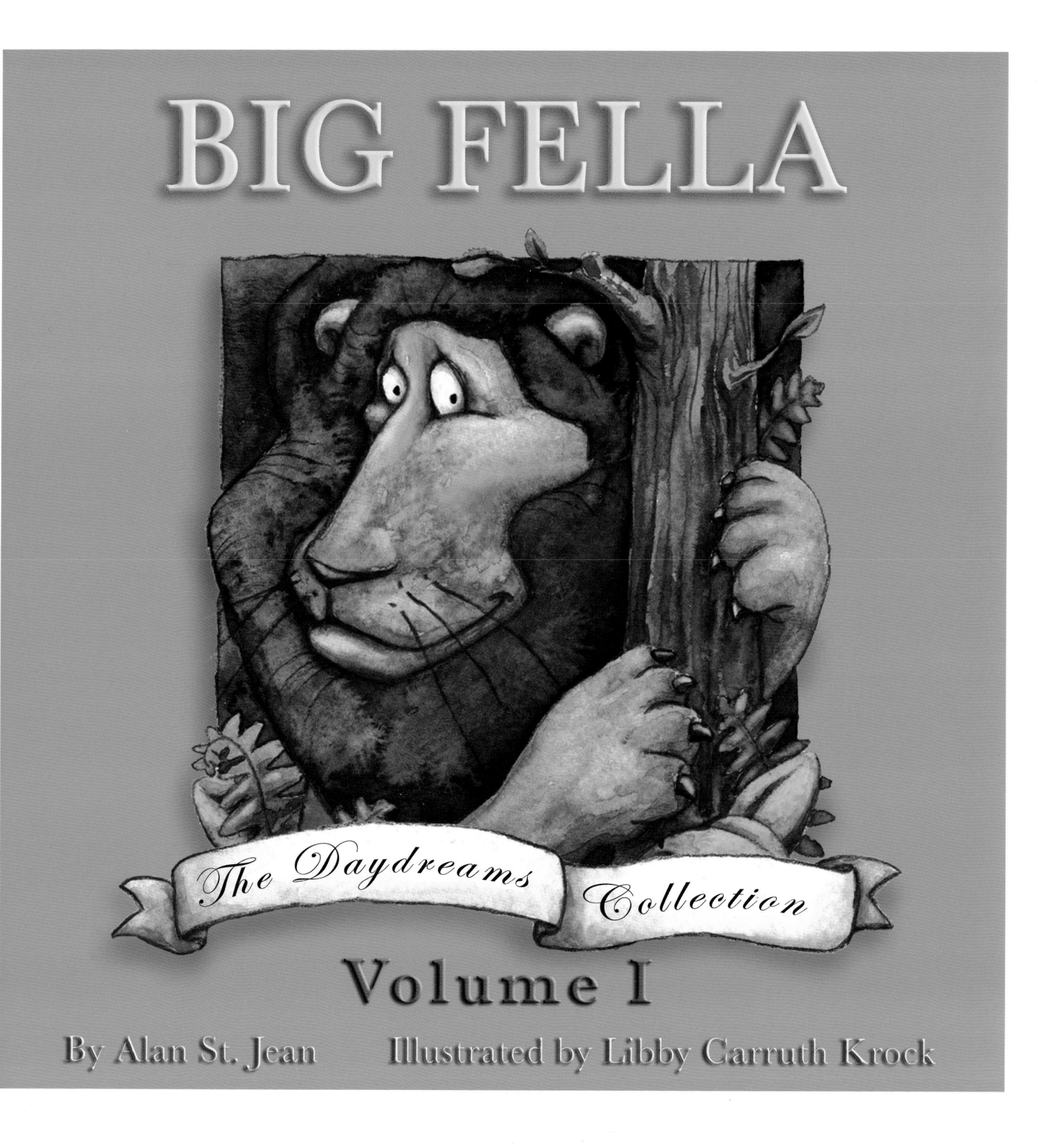

The Daydreams Collection

Volume I

By Alan St. Jean   Illustrated by Libby Carruth Krock

Deep inside the jungle
As dark as it can be,
Ralphie, in his jungle hat
Peeked behind a tree.
He held a shiny compass
In his chubby little hand,
He was looking for a lion,
The BIGGEST in the land.
"Ralphie to the rescue!"
He giggled and he grinned.
Hand held high, he bravely
Put his finger to the wind.
He's heard about this lion,
Big Fella was his name...
A wild, scary, jungle cat
That Ralphie planned to tame.

"Ralphie!" called the teacher,
As Ralphie lost a shoe.
"Can you tell your classmates
What's the sum of two plus two?"
"Big Fella!" Ralphie blurted out,
Still somewhat in a daze.
At once he heard a tapping toe
And saw the teacher's gaze.

"Two plus two is four," the teacher said,
"Just look at you!
Daydreams every day, and now
You've even lost your shoe!"

She softly knelt at Ralphie's side
And whispered in his ear.
"Let's work together. Harmony.
Cooperation here."
The children laughed, the teacher winked
As Ralphie scratched his head.
"What's cooperation? Harmony?
What's what you said?"
"It's like singing," said the teacher,
"When singers sing as one.
Use your imagination,
But wait 'til school is done."

Later on that evening,
At home and in his bed,
Ralphie thought back on the day
And what his teacher said.
"Cooperation, harmony,
When singers sing as one.
Use my imagination?
I think this might be fun!"

Suddenly the room grew dark.
The lamp stand disappeared.
Crickets chirped, grass grew thick,
Things were getting weird.
Something moved behind him.
A zebra, and a yak!
Ralphie touched his jungle hat,
He laughed and yelled, "I'm back!"

With narrowed eyes, a crooked smile,
Compass in his hand,
Ralphie took a great big breath,
Then set out on the land.
He came upon a tree, and heard
Ra-ta-tata-tat.
Looking up he saw a bird.
"What kind of sound is that?"

A funny looking bird it was
With feathers all a clutter,
Stopped its tapping, heaved a sigh,
And then began to mutter.
"Frumpled clothes, a silly hat,
You're somewhat of a bungle.
I tap the tree to play my song,
The best song in the jungle."

Ralphie heard a *blub-blub-blub*,
Then headed through the wood.
He came upon a stream so deep
Inside, three hippos stood!
Hiding underwater
They breathed bubbles through their nose.
With bubbles popping in the air,
A silly song arose.

"Hello!" shouted Ralphie.
"What are all the bubbles for?"
The largest hippo turned and slowly
Floated to the shore.
"Hello to you!" the hippo said,
His tiny tail a quiver.
"The bubbles pop and make a song,
The best song in the river."

And then a sound like angels
Whispered in the air.
Ralphie ran down river
To see what could be there.
He happened on a gathering
Of fifty yellow fish.
With mouths above the water,
They sang quite angelish.

"Hello, what are you doing?"
Asked Ralphie to the school.
"Wait!" He said, "Don't tell me.
You're angel fish! How cool!"

The earth began to rumble,
So Raphie turned around,
Just in time to see giraffes
Run across the ground.
He burst into the clearing
Which scattered lots of birds.
And then, to his amazement,
He heard these funny words:

"Ohweeeoh! Such a Big Fella,
Ohweeeoh! Oh me oh my,
Ohweeeoh! Such a Big Fella,
Ohweeeoh! Gotta run and hide."

"Curious," said Ralphie,
"Somehow you seem afraid.
You're taller than the mountaintops,
And yet you run away?"
"Big Fella!" cried the first giraffe.
"He's somewhere very near!
You better run. Take cover!
Before he bites your ear!"

Ralphie laughed, "I'm not afraid,
Big Fella's just a kitty."
Then he heard another sound,
A sound that sounded witty.

"Who's afraid of lions?"
Said a voice high in a tree.
"I'm the king of jungle land,
So let the beast fear me!"
Ralphie shouted, "Who are you?"
Then, movement in the trees.
He saw a chunky monkey
Who was swinging by his knees!
The monkey stopped and turned around,
A watch was on his wrist.
He flashed a smile, just for a while,
Then swung into the mist.
"Wait for me!" cried Ralphie
As he grabbed a hanging vine.
"Sorry, lad," the monkey said,
"It's nineteen after nine!"
"Nineteen...what...you have a watch?
Please come back!" he shouted.
When there was no answer
Ralphie took a seat and pouted.

"Chunky monkey," Ralphie mumbled,
"Won't cooperate.
Harmony..." the boy jumped up,
"I hope it's not too late!"
Heading back the way he came,
He found the tall giraffes.
"A favor, please," he asked them,
Even though it made them laugh.

He ran back to the river,
To the fifty angel fish.
He asked his real big favor,
They replied they'd grant his wish.

His head down in the water,
Ralphie breathed words in a bubble.
He asked the hippo's for a favor,
The hippos said, "No trouble!"

Ralphie found the cluttered bird
Still tapping in his tree.
He asked him for a favor.
The bird replied, "We'll see."
So all the jungle animals
That made a screech and sound,
Were gathered in the clearing
With the friends that Ralphie found.
Bees that buzzed,
And birds that hummed,
Snakes that hissed,
Elephants that drummed,
Zebras with stripes,
Squirrels that fly,
Rhinos with trumpeting horns,
Oh my!

Ralphie slowly raised his hand
As silence filled the air.
He looked at every creature, but,
Chunky monkey wasn't there.
"We'll have to start without him!"
Ralphie did not hesitate.
"Each of you, for harmony,
I need you to cooperate!"

He pointed to the hippos,
"Go ahead and sing your song!"
So the hippos started blubbing
As the bird tapped right along.
He pointed to the angelfish,
"Start humming anytime!"
Their fifty little voices
Were in tune and right in time!

"Okay, giraffes, don't be afraid,
You knew your time would come!
Lift up your voice, and one more thing,
Make sure you sing as one!"
Then all the creatures great and small
Began to sing a song.
A song born of the jungle,
Where all could join along.

Just as music filled the air,
A voice rang in the trees.
Chunky monkey singing,
He was swinging by his knees!
"Singing, swinging!" Ralphie laughed,
The song turned up a notch.
"I knew he'd finally get here.
Just where did he get that watch?"
They sang the song into the night,
This lesson Ralphie learned:
Cooperation, harmony,
Are something to be earned.
Work real hard, listen well,
Don't leave it up to chance.

And, oh, as for Big Fella,
Well...

He just wants to dance!